The Baby Bunny

by Margaret Hillert
Illustrated by Robert Masheris

DEAR CAREGIVER, The *Beginning-to-Read* series is a carefully written collection of classic readers you may remember from your own childhood. Each book features text comprised of common sight words to provide your child ample practice reading the words that appear most frequently in written text. The many additional details in the pictures enhance the story and offer the opportunity for you to help your child expand oral language and develop comprehension.

Begin by reading the story to your child, followed by letting him or her read familiar words and soon your child will be able to read the story independently. At each step of the way, be sure to praise your reader's efforts to build his or her confidence as an independent reader. Discuss the pictures and encourage your child to make connections between the story and his or her own life. At the end of the story, you will find reading activities and a word list that will help your child practice and strengthen beginning reading skills.

Above all, the most important part of the reading experience is to have fun and enjoy it!

Shannon Cannon

Shannon Cannon,
Literacy Consultant

Norwood House Press • P.O. Box 316598 • Chicago, Illinois 60631
For more information about Norwood House Press please visit our website at
www.norwoodhousepress.com or call 866-565-2900.

LIBRARY OF CONGRESS CATALOGING-IN-PUBLICATION DATA

Hillert, Margaret.
  The baby bunny / Margaret Hillert ; illustrated by Robert Masheris. —
Rev. and expanded library ed.
    p. cm. — (Beginning-to-read series)
  Summary: Easy-to-read text follows the growth, antics, and adventures of a
baby bunny.
  ISBN-13: 978-1-59953-188-5 (library edition : alk. paper)
  ISBN-10: 1-59953-188-7 (library edition : alk. paper) [1.
Rabbits—Fiction.] I. Masheris, Robert, ill. II. Title.
  PZ7.H558Bab 2008
  [E]—dc22   2008001644

Beginning-to-Read series (c) 2009 by Margaret Hillert.
Library edition published by permission of Pearson Education, Inc. in
arrangement with Norwood House Press, Inc. All rights reserved.
This book was originally published by Follett Publishing Company in 1981.

Here is a baby.
Is it a bunny?
No, it is not a bunny.

Here is a baby.
Is it a bunny?
No, it is not a bunny.

Where is the baby bunny?
Do you see it now?
Look, look.
Can you find it?

Oh, yes.
Here it is.
Down in here.
And here is the mother, too.

What a little baby it is.
Can it run?
Can it jump?
No, no.
It is too little.

The bunny wants to eat.
See what the mother can do.
The mother can help.

The mother can do this, too.
See the mother work.
The bunny likes it.

Now see the baby bunny.
It is not too little.
It can come out here.

It can run.
It can jump.
It can play.

Look, look.
The bunny can find something.
The bunny can eat and eat
and eat.

13

And look now.
See what the bunny can do.
This is good.

What will the bunny do now?
Where will the bunny go?
Can you guess?

Away, away.
Up,
  and up,
  and up.

Down,
  down,
    down,
      down,
        down.

What is this?
What can the bunny see?
It looks like the little bunny.

Here is something funny.
It can not run.
It can not run at the bunny.

What will it do?
It will go away now.
Away, away.

Here comes something.
Something big.
Look out, little bunny.
Look out.

Run, run, run.
Get away.
Get away, little bunny.

Oh, here is the mother.
This is good.
The mother can help.

Look at this.
Look in here.
The baby is with the mother.
No one can get the baby bunny now.

The following activities support the findings of the National Reading Panel that determined the most effective components for reading instruction are: Phonemic Awareness, Phonics, Vocabulary, Fluency, and Text Comprehension.

Phonemic Awareness: The /ē/ sound spelled y

Oral Blending: Say the /ē/ sound for your child. Say the following words and ask your child to say the new word made by adding the /ē/ sound to the end:

babe + /ē/ = baby	care + /ē/ = carry	part + /ē/ = party
trick + /ē/ = tricky	bun + /ē/ = bunny	mom + /ē/ = mommy
store + /ē/ = story	dad + /ē/ = daddy	dust + /ē/ = dusty
sleep + /ē/ = sleepy	wind + /ē/ = windy	count + /ē/ = county

Phonics: The letter Yy

1. Demonstrate how to form the letters **Y** and **y** for your child.

2. Have your child practice writing **Y** and **y** at least three times each.

3. Ask your child to point to the words in the book that have the letter **y** in them (either beginning or ending).

4. Write down the following and ask your child to add the letter **y** in the spaces each word:

bab_	bunn_	berr_	happ_	pon_
fort_	an_	penn_	man_	eas_
pupp_	sunn_	kitt_	dais_	chill_

5. Read each word aloud and ask your child to repeat it.

6. Ask your child to independently read as many of the words as possible.

Vocabulary: Baby Animal Names

1. Explain to your child that baby animals often have different names than their parents.

2. Write each of the following words on separate index cards:

rabbit/bunny	squirrel/pup	skunk/kit	tiger/cub
frog/tadpole	cow/calf	pig/piglet	dog/puppy
cat/kitten	duck/duckling	chicken/chick	goat/kid
goose/gosling	kangaroo/joey	deer/fawn	horse/foal

3. Place the adult and baby names next to each other and read the words to your child.

4. Mix up the words.

5. Work with your child to match the adult/baby animal pairs.

Fluency: Choral Reading

1. Reread the story with your child at least two more times while your child tracks the print by running a finger under the words as they are read. Ask your child to read the words he or she knows with you.

2. Reread the story aloud together. Be careful to read at a rate that your child can keep up with.

3. Repeat choral reading and allow your child to be the lead reader and ask him or her to change from a whisper to a loud voice while you follow along and change your voice.

Text Comprehension: Discussion Time

1. Ask your child to retell the sequence of events in the story.

2. To check comprehension, ask your child the following questions:

   • How does the mother rabbit take care of the baby bunny?

   • How do adults take care of you?

   • What does the baby bunny see in the water?

   • What lesson do you think the baby bunny learned?

WORD LIST

The Baby Bunny uses the 51 words listed below.

This list can be used to practice reading the words that appear in the text. You may wish to write the words on index cards and use them to help your child build automatic word recognition. Regular practice with these words will enhance your child's fluency in reading connected text.

a	get	no	up
and	go	not	
at	good	now	want(s)
away	guess		what
		oh	where
baby	help	one	will
big	here	out	with
bunny			work
	in	play	
can	is		yes
come(s)	it	run	you
do	jump	see	
down		something	
	likes		
eat	little	the	
	look(s)	this	
find		to	
funny	mother	too	

ABOUT THE AUTHOR Margaret Hillert has written over 80 books for children who are just learning to read. Her books have been translated into many different languages and over a million children throughout the world have read her books. She first started writing poetry as a child and has continued to write for children and adults throughout her life. A first grade teacher for 34 years, Margaret is now retired from teaching and lives in Michigan where she likes to write, take walks in the morning, and care for her three cats.

Photograph by Glenna Washburn

ABOUT THE ADVISER Shannon Cannon contributed the activities pages that appear in this book. Shannon serves as a literacy consultant and provides staff development to help improve reading instruction. She is a frequent presenter at educational conferences and workshops. Prior to this she worked as an elementary school teacher and as president of a curriculum publishing company.